THE GRUMBLES

A STORY ABOUT GRATITUDE

Written by
TRICIA GOYER
AND **AMY PARKER**

Illustrated by
MONICA DE RIVAS

RP KIDS
PHILADELPHIA

Running Press Kids
Hachette Book Group
1290 Avenue of the Americas, New York, NY 10104
www.runningpress.com/rpkids
@RP_Kids

Printed in China

First Edition: September 2021

Published by Running Press Kids, an imprint of Perseus Books, LLC,
a subsidiary of Hachette Book Group, Inc. The Running Press Kids name
and logo is a trademark of the Hachette Book Group.

The Hachette Speakers Bureau provides a wide range of authors for
speaking events. To find out more, go to www.hachettespeakersbureau.com
or call (866) 376-6591.

The publisher is not responsible for websites (or their content)
that are not owned by the publisher.

Print book cover and interior design by Marissa Raybuck.

Scripture quotation from *The Holy Bible, New International Version®*,
NIV® Copyright © 1973, 1978, 1984, 2011 by Biblica, Inc.®
Used by permission. All rights reserved worldwide.

Library of Congress Control Number: 2020943041

ISBNs: 978-0-7624-7338-0 (hardcover), 978-0-7624-7339-7 (ebook),
978-0-7624-7342-7 (ebook), 978-0-7624-7341-0 (ebook)

APS

10 9 8 7 6 5 4 3 2 1

To my grateful family, whose grumbling started this journey.
–T.G.

To my boys—may we always find something to be grateful for.
–A.P.

To you . . . always grateful!
–M.D.R.

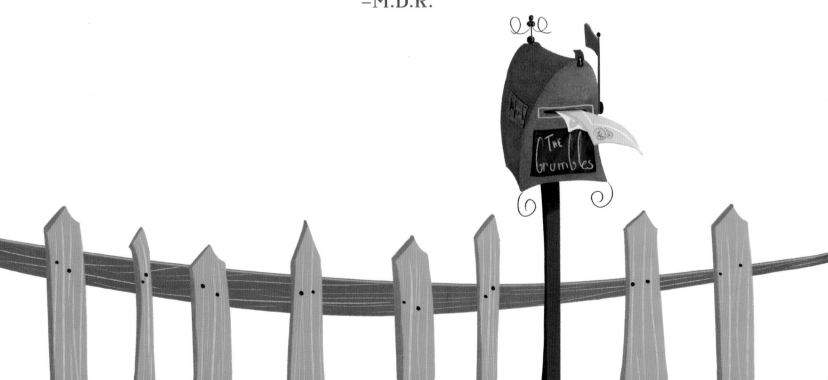

The Grumbles were a happy family.
Most of the time.
Well, a lot of the time.
Okay, *some* of the time.

Daddy Grumble was happy . . .
until he read the water bill.

Mama Grumble was happy . . .
until she saw the laundry.

Brother Grumble was happy . . .
until Sister took too long.

Sister Grumble was happy . . .
until Brother used her stuff.

And Baby Grumble was happy . . .
until she got hungry.

Or wet.

Or tired.

That's when the Grumbles,
well, started to grumble.

Daddy Grumble
would stomp his foot.

Mama Grumble would shake her head.

Brother Grumble would yell and complain.
Sister Grumble would tattle and whine.

And Baby Grumble would
wahhh, wahhh, wahhh.

And then, Grandma Grateful came for a visit.

When Daddy showed her the water bill,
Grandma smiled and laughed.

When Mama pointed at the laundry,
Grandma whistled and sang.

When Sister took too long or
Brother used her stuff, Grandma gave
them both a great big hug.

And when Baby Grumble was tired
or wet or hungry, Grandma rocked
and giggled and cooed.

Grandma was grateful.

After a while, the Grumbles started to think that,
maybe, they could be grateful too.

When Daddy read the water bill,
he thanked God for his job.

When Mama saw the laundry,
she smiled at the kids
who wore all those clothes.

When Sister took too long,
Brother whistled and waited.

When Brother used her stuff,
Sister helped to show him how.

And when Baby was
hungry or wet or tired . . .

well, she still cried.

But that was okay.

Because the Grumbles
were all
grateful.

Most of the time.

NOTE TO PARENTS:

Does your family sometimes have the grumbles?
Grumbles are more than words.
Talk to your kids about each person's grumble style.
Which style matches which person in your family?

Muttering	Pouting	Whining
Stomping	Scowling	Crying

The best way to stop grumbles is to do what
Grandma Grateful did: model gratitude.
As we adults model our gratefulness,
our kids will catch on.
And when kids are caught being
grateful with your praise and encouragement,
they are sure to repeat the behavior!